OL' PAUL
The Mighty Logger

OL' PAUL

The Mighty Logger

Being a True Account of the Seemingly
Incredible Exploits and Inventions of the
GREAT PAUL BUNYAN, Profusely
Illustrated with Drawings Made at the
Scene by the Author, GLEN ROUNDS,
and Now Republished in This Special
FORTIETH ANNIVERSARY Edition.

HOLIDAY HOUSE

New York   1976

Contents

Ol' Paul and His Camp

For many years there have come drifting out of the timber country strange tales of a giant logger and inventor, Paul Bunyan by name. He is said to have been the inventor of logging. At night, around the pot-bellied bunkhouse stoves in the lumber camps, around campfires of road construction crews, and even in the hobo jungles, I have heard the stories of his great strength and wonderful inventions told and retold.

But most of these stories are based on hearsay alone, so of course can't be depended on to give the true facts. Such as the story that he kept his great beard in a buckskin bag made from the skins of seventy-seven deer, and took it out only on odd Sundays and legal holidays to comb it. The truth of the matter is that the bag was made of the skins of one hundred and sixteen elk, and he wore it only at night, to keep catamounts and such from bedding down in his whiskers.

So I feel it is my duty to write down the *true* story of Paul Bunyan, and illustrate it with the drawings I made during the three winters I worked for him.

Some of these stories you may find a mite hard to believe, but you must remember that folks who do things that are easy to believe don't often have stories told about them, anyway.

Not much is known of Ol' Paul's childhood. He never spoke about it to me, and having been raised in a country where it was considered bad form, not to say downright unhealthy, to be too curious about a man's past, I never asked.

But from chance remarks he dropped from time to time and from old Indian legends, I think it is safe to suppose that he was born of French-Canadian parents somewhere near the headwaters of the St. Lawrence River. He seems to have been a mighty husky shaver from the first. There is a story that when but two weeks

old he caught and strangled with his bare hands a full-grown grizzly bear. And one day, while playing by the river, he fell in. When fished out by the neighbors, there were found caught in his long beard, which he is said to have had from birth, some sixteen or seventeen beaver. This pleased his father more than somewhat, the pelts bringing him a mighty nice sum.

At the age of three months he had outgrown his parents' cabin, and the neighbors were complaining about the damage he was doing to fences and timber as he played among the little farms. So he packed his clothes in a warbag and, telling his folks good-bye, went way back in the hills to a great cave he knew of. Here he spent his time growing up and inventing hunting and fishing.

When next heard of, he was a man grown, had already invented logging, and somewhere had found Babe, the Mighty Blue Ox, who was his constant companion. As for the size of the Ox, it is said that one hundred and seventy-one axe handles, three small cans of tomatoes, and a plug of chewing tobacco laid end to end would exactly equal the distance between his eyes. So you can figure just how big he must have been.

At first Ol' Paul carried on his logging in a small way, felling the trees himself, and having Babe skid them to the river. But as time went on he invented newer and better ways of doing things, and his fame began to spread. Soon others took advantage of his having invented logging and went into the business themselves, thereby inventing competition. But as the stories of his almost unbelievable doings spread, men fell over themselves to work for him. To be able to say you'd once worked for Ol' Paul marked you as a real he-coon among loggers, and before long he had a picked crew, the like of which has never been seen since.

There was Ole, the Big Swede, probably the best blacksmith the woods have ever seen, who could shoe six horses at one time, holding them in his lap like puppies the while.

And Shot Gunderson, the woods boss, who could swing a double-bitted axe in each hand and fell four trees at a time. He was quite a hand to chew snuff, and I once saw him knock a wildcat out of the top of a bull pine with one squirt of tobacco juice.

Sourdough Sam, the camp cook, invented sourdough flapjacks, which became the favorite breakfast in Paul's camps, although they set a trifle heavy on any but the most rugged stomachs.

Hot Biscuit Slim, Sourdough's assistant, did all the rest of the cooking, not being a breakfast specialist. He was a mournful-looking duck, who never spoke except on cloudy Thursdays.

And in later years there was Johnny Inkslinger, who did the bookkeeping, and figured so fast that it took a bucket brigade of thirty men to keep his inkwell filled.

When I first saw Ol' Paul's camp, it was so big that the

Indians who came in to pick over the leavings back of the cookshack often got lost and had to have search parties sent out for them.

Sam's cookshack itself was over two miles long. One whole side was taken up by the great griddle, on which he fried the sourdough flapjacks for which he was famous. It kept a whole bunkhouse full of cookees busy hauling wood for it. The batter was mixed in a big reservoir Paul had dug on a hill back of camp. The mixing was done with an old river steamboat which was kept busy steaming back and forth all night across the lake of sourdough. When the breakfast whistle blew, the floodgates were opened and the batter poured through a flume to a sprinkler system that squirted the cakes on the griddle.

Flunkies with sides of bacon strapped to their boots skated over the smoking surface, greasing it and turning the flapjacks with scoop shovels. As fast as they were done they were stacked on wagons drawn by four horses, which galloped to the mess hall, up a ramp, and down

the middle of the great table, while men with cant hooks rolled the cakes off onto the plates. Another four-horse outfit, hitched to a sprinkler wagon, followed close behind with the syrup. The tables were so long that by the time a wagon reached the end it was nearly noon, so they loaded up with salt and pepper and on the return trip filled the shakers for supper, getting back to the cookshack at ten minutes to six.

Naturally, with a crew of that size using ordinary bunkhouses, the camp would have spread out so that Paul would never have been able to keep track of it. So he built the bunkhouses in interlocking sections, like beehives, and set them in stacks, one on top of the other. After supper he would take the sections down and let the men in, then pile them up again. In warm weather he left them outside, but when it got cold he stacked them up in his office.

These men, I'm right proud to say, were friends of mine, and of all the oddments in my warbag, I think the thing I set most store by is the letter of recommendation Ol' Paul gave me when I left, informing whoever it concerned that I was probably the biggest liar he'd ever had in camp.

Glen Rounds

The Whistling River

It seems that some years before the winter of the Blue Snow (which every old logger remembers because of a heavy fall of bright blue snow which melted to ink, giving folks the idea of writing stories like these, so they tell) Ol' Paul was logging on what was then known as the Whistling River. It got its name from the fact that every morning, right on the dot, at nineteen minutes after five, and every night at ten minutes past six, it r'ared up to a height of two hundred and seventy-three feet and let loose a whistle that could be heard for a distance of six hundred and three miles in any direction.

Of course, if one man listening by himself can hear that far, it seems reasonable to suppose that two men

listening together can hear it just twice as far. They tell me that even as far away as Alaska, most every camp had from two to four whistle-listeners (as many as were needed to hear the whistle without straining), who got two bits a listen and did nothing but listen for the right time, especially quitting time.

However, it seems that the river was famous for more than its whistling, for it was known as the orneriest river that ever ran between two banks. It seemed to take a fiendish delight in tying whole rafts of good saw logs into more plain and fancy knots than forty-three old sailors even knew the names of. It was an old "side winder" for fair. Even so, it is unlikely that Ol' Paul would ever have bothered with it, if it had left his beard alone.

It happened this way. It seems that Ol' Paul is sitting on a low hill one afternoon, combing his great curly beard with a pine tree, while he plans his winter operations. All of a sudden like, and without a word of warning, the river h'ists itself up on its hind legs and squirts about four thousand five hundred and nineteen gallons of river water straight in the center of Ol' Paul's whiskers.

Naturally Paul's considerably startled, but says nothing, figuring that if he pays it no mind, it'll go 'way and leave him be. But no sooner does he get settled back with his thinking and combing again, than the durn river squirts some more! This time, along with the water, it throws in for good measure a batch of mud turtles, thirteen large carp, a couple of drowned muskrat, and half a raft of last year's saw logs. By this time Ol' Paul is pretty mad, and he jumps up and lets loose a yell that causes a landslide out near Pike's Peak, and startles a barber in Missouri so he cuts half the hair off the minister's toupee, causing somewhat of a stir thereabouts. Paul stomps around waving his arms for a spell, and allows:

"By the Gee-Jumpin' John Henry and the Great Horn Spoon, I'll tame that river or bust a gallus tryin'."

He goes over to another hill and sits down to think out a way to tame a river, forgetting his winter operations entirely. He sits there for three days and forty-seven hours without moving, thinking at top speed all the while, and finally comes to the conclusion that the best thing to do is to take out the kinks. But he knows that taking the kinks out of a river as tricky as this one is apt to be quite a chore, so he keeps on sitting there while he figures out ways and means. Of course, he could dig a new channel and run the river through that, but that was never Paul's way. He liked to figure out new ways of doing things, even if they were harder.

Meanwhile he's gotten a mite hungry, so he hollers down to camp for Sourdough Sam to bring him up a little popcorn, of which he is very fond. So Sam hitches up a four-horse team while his helpers are popping the corn, and soon arrives at Paul's feet with a wagon load.

Paul eats popcorn and thinks. The faster he thinks the faster he eats and the faster he eats the faster he thinks, until finally his hands are moving so fast that nothing shows but a blur, and they make a wind that is uprooting trees all around him. His chewing sounds like a couple hundred coffee grinders all going at once. In practically no time at all the ground for three miles and a quarter in every direction is covered to a depth of eighteen inches with popcorn scraps, and several thousand small birds and animals, seeing the ground all white and the air filled with what looks like snowflakes, conclude that a blizzard is upon them and immediately freeze to death, furnishing the men with pot pies for some days.

But to get back to Ol' Paul's problem. Just before the

popcorn is all gone, he decides that the only practical solution is to hitch Babe, the Mighty Blue Ox, to the river and let him yank it straight.

Babe was so strong that he could pull mighty near anything that could be hitched to him. His exact size, as I said before, is not known, for although it is said that he stood ninety-three hands high, it's not known whether that meant ordinary logger's hands, or hands the size of Paul's, which, of course, would be something else again.

However, they tell of an eagle that had been in the habit of roosting on the tip of Babe's right horn, suddenly deciding to fly to the other. Columbus Day, it was, when he started. He flew steadily, so they say, night and day, fair weather and foul, until his wing feathers were worn down to pinfeathers and a new set grew to replace them. In all, he seems to have worn out seventeen sets of feathers on the trip, and from reaching up to brush the sweat out of his eyes so much, had worn all the feathers off the top of his head, becoming completely bald, as are all of his descendants to this day. Finally the courageous bird won through, reaching the brass ball on the tip of the left horn on the seventeenth of March. He waved a wing weakly at the cheering lumberjacks and 'lowed as how he'd of made it sooner but for the head winds.

But the problem is how to hitch Babe to the river, as it's a well-known fact that an ordinary log chain and skid hook will not hold water. So after a light lunch of three sides of barbecued beef, half a wagon load of potatoes, carrots and a few other odds and ends, Ol' Paul goes down to the blacksmith shop and gets Ole, the Big Swede, to help him look through the big instruction book that came with the woods and tells how to do most everything under the sun. But though Paul reads the book through from front to back twice while Ole reads it from back to front, and they both read it once from bottom to top, they find nary a word about how to hook onto a river. However, they do find an old almanac stuck between the pages and get so busy reading up on the weather for the coming year, and a lot of fancy ailments of one kind and another that it's supper time before they know it, and the problem's still unsolved. So Paul decides that the only practical thing to do is to invent a rigging of some kind himself.

At any rate he has to do something, as every time he hears the river whistle, it makes him so mad he's fit to be tied, which interferes with his work more than something. No one can do their best under such conditions.

Being as how this was sort of a special problem, he thought it out in a special way. Paul was like that. As he always thought best when he walked, he had the men survey a circle about thirty miles in diameter to walk around. This was so that if he was quite a while thinking it out, he wouldn't be finding himself way down in Australia when he'd finished.

When everything is ready, he sets his old fur cap tight on his head, clasps his hands behind him, and starts walking and thinking. He thinks and walks. The faster he walks the faster he thinks. He makes a complete circle every half hour. By morning he's worn a path that is knee-deep even on him, and he has to call the men to herd the stock away and keep them from falling in and getting crippled. Three days later he thinks it out, but he's worn himself down so deep that it takes a day and a half to get a ladder built that will reach down that far. When he does get out, he doesn't even wait for breakfast, but whistles for Babe and tears right out across the hills to the north.

The men have no idea what he intends to do, but they know from experience that it'll be good, so they cheer till their throats are so sore they have to stay around the mess hall drinking Paul's private barrel of cough syrup till supper time. And after that they go to bed and sleep very soundly.

Paul and the Ox travel plenty fast, covering twenty-

four townships at a stride, and the wind from their pass-
ing raises a dust that doesn't even begin to settle for
some months. There are those who claim that the pres-
ent dust storms are nothing more or less than that same
dust just beginning to get back to earth—but that's a
matter of opinion. About noon, as they near the North
Pole, they begin to see blizzard tracks, and in a short
time are in the very heart of their summer feeding
grounds. Taking a sack from his shoulder, Paul digs out
materials for a box trap, which he sets near a well-traveled
blizzard trail, and baits with fresh icicles from the top
of the North Pole. Then he goes away to eat his lunch,
but not until he's carefully brushed out his tracks—a
trick he later taught the Indians.

After lunch he amuses himself for a while by throwing
huge chunks of ice into the water for Babe to retrieve,
but he soon has to whistle the great beast out, as every
time he jumps into the water he causes such a splash that

a tidal wave threatens Galveston, Texas, which at that time was inhabited by nobody in particular. Some of the ice he threw in is still floating around the ocean, causing plenty of excitement for the iceberg patrol.

About two o'clock he goes back to his blizzard trap and discovers that he has caught seven half-grown blizzards and one grizzled old nor'wester, which is raising considerable fuss and bids fair to trample the young ones before he can get them out. But he finally manages to get a pair of half-grown ones in his sack and turns the others loose.

About midnight he gets back to camp, and hollers at Ole, the Big Swede:

"Build me the biggest log chain that's ever been built, while I stake out these dad-blasted blizzards! We're goin' to warp it to 'er proper, come mornin'."

Then he goes down to the foot of the river and pickets one of the blizzards to a tree on the bank, then crosses and ties the other directly opposite. Right away the river begins to freeze. In ten minutes the slush ice reaches nearly from bank to bank, and the blizzards are not yet really warmed to their work, either. Paul watches for a few minutes, and then goes back to camp to warm up, feeling mighty well satisfied with the way things are working out.

In the morning the river has a tough time r'aring up for what it maybe knows to be its last whistle, for its foot is frozen solid for more than seventeen miles. The blizzards have really done the business.

By the time breakfast is over, the great chain's ready and Babe all harnessed. Paul quick-like wraps one end of the chain seventy-two times around the foot of the river, and hitches Babe to the other. Warning the men to stand clear, he shouts at the Ox to pull. But though the great beast strains till his tongue hangs out, pulling the chain out into a solid bar some seven and a half miles long, and sinks knee-deep in the solid rock, the river stubbornly refuses to budge, hanging onto its kinks like a snake in a gopher hole. Seeing this, Ol' Paul grabs the chain and, letting loose a holler that blows the tarpaper off the shacks in the Nebraska sandhills, he and the Ox together give a mighty yank that jerks the river loose from end to end, and start hauling it out across the prairie so fast that it smokes.

After a time Paul comes back and sights along the river, which now is as straight as a gun barrel. But he

doesn't have long to admire his work, for he soon finds he has another problem on his hands. You see, it's this way. A straight river is naturally much shorter than a crooked one, and now all the miles and miles of extra river that used to be in the kinks are running wild out on the prairie. This galls the farmers in those parts more than a little. So it looks like Paul had better figure something out, and mighty soon at that, for already he can see clouds of dust the prairie folks are raising as they come at top speed to claim damages.

After three minutes of extra deep thought he sends a crew to camp to bring his big cross-cut saw and a lot of baling wire. He saws the river into nine-mile lengths and the men roll it up like linoleum and tie it with the wire. Some say he used these later when he logged off the desert, rolling out as many lengths as he needed to float his logs. But that's another story.

But his troubles with the Whistling River were not all over. It seems that being straightened sort of took the

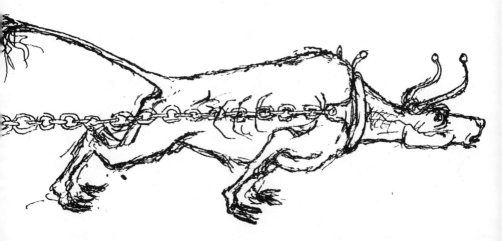

gimp out of the river, and from that day on it refused to whistle even a bird call. And as Paul had gotten into the habit of depending on the whistle to wake up the men in the morning, things were a mite upset.

First he hired an official getter-upper who rode through the camp on a horse, and beat a triangle. But the camp was so big that it took three hours and seventy-odd minutes to make the trip. Naturally some of the men were called too early and some too late. It's hard to say what might have happened if Squeaky Swanson hadn't showed up about that time. His speaking voice was a thin squeak, but when he hollered he could be heard clear out to Kansas on a still day. So every morning he stood outside the cookshack and hollered the blankets off every bunk in camp. Naturally the men didn't stay in bed long after the blankets were off them, what with the cold wind and all, so Squeaky was a great success and for years did nothing but holler in the mornings.

The Bedcats

Ol' Paul had quite a time with the Bedcats one winter, when he was using one of his old camps that had stood deserted for thirty years or more. It happened this way. As every one knows, most bunkhouses have a certain number of bedbugs. These don't annoy a real lumberjack to amount to anything, although you'll hear the greenhorns holler plenty when they first come into camp. But they either make friends with the little beasts or they don't last long. The story is that the loggers all had their pet bugs that followed them around camp and out in the woods like dogs, some even being trained, it is said, to steal blankets off adjoining bunks for their masters on especially cold nights. However, that is as it may be; I never saw it.

But it is a well-known fact that the intelligent little beasts always knew when camp was to be moved, and the night before would come out of wherever they were in the habit of staying and climb into the bedding rolls so as not to be left behind. Then when the new camp was set up, there they were, jumping up and down with excitement to greet the men when they came in from their first day's work.

One time, though, they got fooled. That was the time the Indian, Squatting Calf, comes running into camp just after breakfast with the news that gold has been discovered in the Black Hills. Right away all the men tear out over the hills without even waiting to pick up their blankets. Within three minutes the camp is as empty as an old maid's letter box on Valentine's Day. That night at sundown the little bugs are all lined up at the bunkhouse door waiting for the men to come home as usual. But they don't come.

Ol' Paul's in town at the time, and when he hears the news, he knows there's no use figuring on logging till the gold fever passes, so he goes on a timber cruising trip. He locates some fine timber down Kansas way, and when he finds his men ready to work, he starts a new camp there, as he has a ready market for his lumber in the new

gold towns. And, what with one thing and another, it's about thirty years before he comes back to the old camp. But when he does, he finds trouble waiting for him.

He and the men get there about noon and start cleaning out the old buildings. They're a little surprised to find the bunks filled up with the bones of rabbits and other small animals, but suppose that owls or bobcats have been living there. By night the camp is ready, and after supper the men turn in early. Ol' Paul suddenly wakes up, hearing wild yells and snarls from the bunkhouse, and comes running out of his office to see the men clawing over one another in their underwear, trying to get out in the open. They swear that their bunks are full of wildcats which have been crawling all over them. Now Paul knows wildcats, and he's never heard of one that'll come within a hundred yards of a logger if it has its 'druthers. As he can find nothing in there when he looks, he figures that being as it's the day after payday, the men have probably eaten something that disagrees with them. But they won't go back in the bunkhouse, so he lets them sleep in the stables that night.

But the next night the same thing happens, so Paul decides to get his pistol and sleep in the bunkhouse himself. When a bunch of lumberjacks are scared to sleep in

a place there must be something wrong somewhere. For a time things are quiet enough to suit anybody, and Paul finally decides that the men have been reading too many old mystery magazines, and dozes off. But he wakes up mighty soon. What feels like a couple of full-grown wildcats seem to have gotten tangled up in his beard, and his blanket is heaving around like he has a runaway cat show under it. The whole bunk is full of animals of some kind, hissing and snarling like all get out. It's none too comfortable there, but Ol' Paul doesn't lose his head. He grabs out in the dark and gets a couple of the beasts and stuffs them into a sack he's got handy. Of course as soon as he starts floundering around the things clear out, like any wild animal, and by the time the men come running with lanterns the place is quiet again.

They carefully open up the sack to see what they've caught. The animals inside are not bobcats. In fact, nobody has ever seen anything like them. They are the size of bobcats, but they have several pairs of legs. They are covered with a heavy coat of reddish-brown fur, which is quite long on the back, but due to the shortness of their

legs, is worn down to the length of plush on the bottom. Naturally Paul and the men are more than a little puzzled.

It is not until the Indians come into camp that they find out what it is they have caught. The Indians call them Bedcats, and from them Paul learns the story.

It seems that the little bugs, being left alone in camp, had to forage for themselves. At first many died, but the stronger ones survived and grew larger, soon attacking small mice and sparrows. As the years passed, they grew fur to keep them warm, and became more and more savage, each generation a little larger and wilder than the one before. Eventually they were bringing in gophers and small rabbits to feed their young. Later, it seems, they crossed with bobcats and the half-breeds were really fierce hunters. They took to running in packs like wolves, baying at the moon, and in a pitched fight a full-grown bobcat was no match for even an ordinary-sized Bedcat. The Indians set deadfalls for them, and made warm fur robes and mittens from the pelts. But with the return of the lumberjacks, some forgotten instinct seemed to urge them into the blankets in the bunks, which upset even the soundest sleepers.

Something had to be done. Ol' Paul buys the Indians a lot of number four wolf traps and offers a five-dollar bounty for the scalps, so they are soon trapped out. I haven't heard of any quite that big being seen since.

The Moaning Boots

The winter Ol' Paul logged on the southwest slope of the Rock Candy Mountain he got a hoodoo in camp. Everyone knows that this sometimes happens, and when it does, nothing can be done about it. This particular hoodoo was in a pair of Ol' Paul's boots. It seems he was needing a new pair, so as usual he ships a train load of bull hides to Rhode Island to be made up. That spring, just before he's ready to move camp, he gets word that they're at the railroad, loaded on two flat cars. So he goes over and gets them. They're a fine pair of boots, but from the very beginning they're strange. For one thing, they never need breaking in, as such boots usually do, and their habit of running from their place by the stove to the side of Paul's bunk in the mornings causes more than one set of goose pimples! There is considerable muttering among the men, and talk that a workman slipped while the insole was being laid, and got glued flat between that and the bottom one, spooking the boots. But Paul claims he's often had boots that did things like that and there's nothing to the story. For a while nothing happens that seems to be out of the way.

In the meantime the camp is broken up and Paul takes a small crew that's going to work all summer and goes into the Rock Candy country to start grubbing out tote roads and build a new camp.

The second night after they've set up a temporary camp, the boots are laying beside the fire between one of Hot Biscuit Slim's dutch ovens and the big coffee pot, when all of a sudden like, they roll over on their sides and start the most gosh-awful moaning. Paul sets up and allows he'll be nibbled to death by ducks if that's not the queerest thing he's seen in some time. The men's eyes are popping out so you can knock them off with a stick, and even Hot Biscuit Slim, who's noted for never saying anything but a growl, says "Hurumph!", which startles the men almost as much as the moaning of the boots, as his voice is somewhat rusty from not being used. For a bit nothing happens except that the boots keep moaning and the men all seem to have gotten on the other side of the fire in practically no time.

Then a commotion breaks out in the corral where the oxen are, and everybody tears out in that direction, it being a fine excuse to get away from the boots. Then they wish they hadn't been in such a hurry, for they see one of the oxen being hauled away by a pair of the biggest mosquitoes they've ever seen. The woods often grow mosquitoes that seem plenty big, but these have a wing spread of about sixteen feet, and seem to have raided corrals before.

They worked this way. Two of them carried a sling like those used to get a crippled ox off the ground. The others acted as scouts and cut the doomed critter out from the rest of the herd. As soon as they had him in the clear, one of the sling carriers would fold his wings and dive under the ox's belly, carrying the end of the sling with him. When he was in the air again, the two flew in a

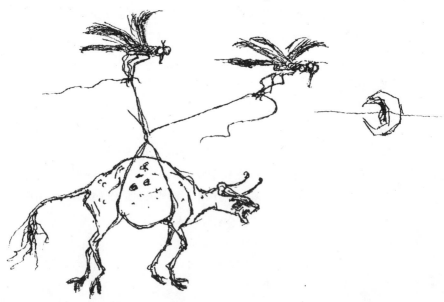

figure eight to tie up the ends, and sailed off with the fat beef dangling below.

Naturally this doesn't do much towards cheering the men up, but Paul sets a guard over the corrals and the rest of the night passes without anything happening. The next day they clean out a cave nearby and fit it with a heavy door. At sundown they drive the oxen inside and move the cook fire there as well.

But early in the evening the boots start moaning again, and soon they hear a sound they swear is made by somebody with a diamond drill and double jack drilling in the rock. Some of the bolder of the men crawl out another entrance and see a hair-raising sight. The huge mosquitoes are at work, drilling a shaft through the rock towards the cave. One holds his bill against the rock while two more hit him on the head with their tails. It's really quite a sight, the strikers working together like expert hard-rock men, and the sparks flying when the tempered steel of the bills bites the stone. Already they've gone six feet into the granite, but Ol' Paul, being an expert geologist, knows that they'll strike a ten-foot vein of quartz soon. This will slow them up, as their bills will have to be sharpened every ten minutes, and the nearest sandstone outcrop is over in Minnesota. By the time they fly over there to sharpen up, it'll be near morning, so he figures he has time to think out a way to fix them.

By morning he has a plan. Nearby is an abandoned sawmill. Paul has the men haul the old boiler out into the open and has the flues cut out of the inside. That afternoon he leads an old ox into the boiler, and he and Ole, the Big Swede, take a sledge apiece and go in too, and shut the door.

That night for the third time the boots start moaning, and sure enough, they soon hear the giant mosquitoes drilling away at the boiler plate, trying to get at the ox. In about ten minutes the bills start breaking through. As fast as one comes through, Paul and Ole bend it over with the sledges. This of course puts that particular mosquito out of commission, as he can't get away. At the end of two hours they have the entire flock riveted to the boiler. They just sit down to wipe the sweat out of their eyes and figure what they'd better do next, when the boots start moaning once more. By now they know that's a sign of trouble, so they jerk the door open and look out in time to see the ground floating away from under them. They jump mighty fast, before they're high enough to get damaged. It seems that the mosquitoes know they're trapped, and decide to fly away, boiler and all. They're soon out of sight, and for that matter, as far as I know, that's the last that's ever been heard of them.

Paul and the men go ahead with the tote roads, and finally they're ready to start building the bunkhouses and cookshacks. Paul starts out with a crew to fell timber for the buildings, and for the first time in three weeks, the boots start moaning. The men want to go back to camp right away, but no one wants to be the first to say so, and Paul seems not to notice, so they go on.

He picks out a tree and tells the men to go to work. But the minute they unsling their axes every tree within a stone's throw disappears into the ground like a woodchuck into a burrow, and can't be coaxed up, any way. This, you may be sure, is a mite unusual, and causes considerable head-scratching. Then they decide to try sneaking up and taking the trees by surprise. But if they do succeed in sinking an ax into a tree, right away it drops into its burrow, jerking the ax out of the man's hands. One fellow nearly follows his axe, being a trifle slow letting loose. Naturally Ol' Paul can't afford to be losing axes like that, or men either, for that matter. After some scouting which convinces them that all the trees hereabouts have burrows, they go back to camp for dinner.

Paul doesn't say much, but he spends the afternoon oiling his big seventy-six barreled shotgun and rifle combined. In the meantime he's had Ole, the Big Swede, making a pile of ten-foot crowbars.

Next morning before breakfast he loads each barrel with six of these and goes out to the timber. The trees not being gun shy, they stand quietly sunning themselves at the tops of their burrows while he sights the seventy-six barrels. He aims in such a way that each barrel is lined on six trees. When he finally pulls all seventy-six triggers at once the country is so startled that there isn't even an echo. Ol' Paul comes back for breakfast while the dust and smoke settle. Afterwards, when the men follow him out with their axes, they find he's shot the crowbars through the trees so that they stick out three feet on each side of the trunk. They can't get into their burrows and the men have no trouble in felling them. Paul gets six trees with each barrel, so you can figure that they have all they can fell and skid into camp that day.

All winter they work that way, Ol' Paul going out before breakfast and shooting the trees. After he starts work with the full crew he often has to take four or five shots to get enough for a day's work. The trees get mighty gun shy, too, so he's often late for breakfast. But it's about the finest timber he's seen in years, so he doesn't mind.

The boots don't moan again until just before the spring breakup, although they whimpered a little just before Sourdough Sam's Whiskers got caught in the oven door. But one night in early April they break out moaning in real earnest, and the next morning it rains. But not a usual kind of rain; this one falls straight up. The boots were right, when they moaned for trouble. Naturally, never expecting rain that'd fall up instead of down, Ol' Paul had seen to it that the roofs were tight, but the floors all had wide cracks in them.

So of course they leak. Soon the bunks are soaked and water stands two feet deep on the ceilings, and is getting deeper all the time. The men have to work lively to chop holes in the roofs to let the rain out before it gets down to the windows and pushes them out. Over in the cook-shacks the floors leak so bad there's no chance to get anything but cold sourdough biscuits for breakfast, and as the men sit at the tables in the mess halls, the rain runs up their pantlegs and up their sleeves, making them very much disgusted with things in general.

For a week this keeps up, until the news of it spreads even back East and a professor starts out to write it up for the papers. By the time he gets there, however, it's stopped, and as the big breakup has come everybody is too busy with the log drive to say more than howdy. That's probably the reason so few people ever have heard of the rain that fell straight up, or believed it if they did hear.

But after that the men refused to work for Paul unless he got rid of the boots, as they figured they were the cause of all the trouble they'd been having, not realizing that the boots moaned only because trouble was on the way. Being a reasonable man, Ol' Paul left the boots in town and only wore them when he played poker with Sowbelly Burke. Whenever Burke even thought of pulling a card from his sleeve or from the bottom of the deck, the boots would start moaning, so the games were kept pretty clean. The moaning upset Burke so much that Paul usually came out ahead, winning steadily all that summer.

Paul Goes Hunting

Ol' Paul was a great hunter, and as everyone knows, hunting is not much fun without a dog. But Paul traveled so fast when he hunted that the toughest dog was worn down to nothing but a puppy after a single day of trying to keep up with him. So one summer, when work was tolerable light, Ol' Paul set himself to solve this problem.

First he wrote his good friend P. T. Barnum to send him a bird dog, but was more than a little disappointed when the dog came to find that it couldn't fly. However, he spent all summer, spare times, teaching it to ride a bicycle. This was quite a chore, but he had considerable fun with the folks thereabouts, watching their eyes pop as he took great strides across the prairie with the dog on his bicycle, his long, silky ears flying in the wind, pedaling along behind. But when it came to hunting, the bicycle was useless in the brush and fallen timber, so finally Paul sent the dog back to Barnum, where he was quite an attraction.

About that time one of the men came into camp with a pup he'd picked up somewhere. The little rascal wasn't much to look at; seemed to be half Dachshund and half Wolfhound, which gave him a high-behind appearance. Ol' Paul got an idea. He bought the dog and took over the care and feeding of it himself. He had a desk in his office that had a six-inch space under it, and under there was where he always fed the pup. When he filled the plate he'd shove it just exactly halfway back. Naturally Skookum, as he was named, would run under to eat, with half his back and his hind quarters out in the room.

Ol' Paul fed him nothing but sourdough pancakes and beef stew. As everybody knows, sourdough swells plenty, causing the pup to grow fast to keep up with it.

He couldn't help himself. As he was fed every ten minutes during the day and every seventeen minutes during the night, he spent practically all his time with his front quarters under the desk. Naturally they didn't have room to grow much, while his hind quarters were left free to grow as fast as they liked. In three weeks he had gained seventy-nine pounds and was still growing, and at the age of two months was full grown. He was still six inches high in the front, but stood sixteen feet high behind. Naturally, with a build like that, he was always running downhill, even when he was going uphill. So no matter how far or how fast Ol' Paul traveled, Skookum followed him without the least trouble, coming in at night as fresh as a daisy.

One day Paul takes Skookum and his famous seventy-six barreled shotgun and rifle combined and goes hunting. He's hoping to get a Flu-flu bird. This was a rare bird that was always being heard of but seldom seen by reliable people. According to reports it had a head like a turkey and a long bottle-green neck covered with scales the size and colors of dimes. Its wings didn't match, the left being red or pink in color, and the right a dull black. It always flew backwards, never looking where it was going, but looking back towards where it had come from.

Ol' Paul and Skookum hunt for some time, without seeing any signs of a Flu-flu bird. After a spell they come across a fresh moose trail, and start to follow that. But after a mile and three-quarters, the trail disappears completely. This puzzles Paul more than somewhat, as he's the inventor of tracking and has never lost a trail before. After looking round a bit, they find a bear trail that looks mighty promising, so they start following that. First, however, he stops and polishes his sighting mirrors. You see, the seventy-six barrels are arranged to point in all directions, and he's rigged a complicated set of mirrors so that he can aim all seventy-six barrels at once. He's really loaded for bear.

But after another mile and three-quarters he loses the bear trail, and finds the moose trail again. This goes on for several hours, the trail changing every mile and three-quarters, until Paul gets so upset he's about ready to think he's seeing things. Luckily, he catches up with the end of the trail at the edge of a small swamp, and finds an animal of some kind mired down in the mud. He reaches down and gets it.

Although Ol' Paul has seen many strange things in his day, he'll be "teetotally jam switched if this isn't the beatinest yet." The beast has a head like a fox, except that its ears are much bigger and kind of floppy. Its shoulders and forelegs are those of a moose, but its hind legs stick up in the air, instead of down, and have the feet of a cinnamon bear. For trimming it has a long, hairless tail like a possum's, only much larger. It seems its habit was to walk a mile and three-quarters on the moose legs and then turn over and walk on the bear legs. This was so confusing to hunters that nobody had ever seen one before.

Ol' Paul looks at the thing for a while, and finally decides to name it a Bear-behind. Then he turns it loose, figuring he'll catch one nearer camp some time to show the men. But he never did.

The Whirling Whimpus

All the animals Ol' Paul found were not as useless as the Bear-behind. The Whirling Whimpus, for instance, was a very peculiar beast he found the winter he was logging on the other side of the River That Ran Sidewise.

Nobody knows just what a full-grown Whimpus looked like, because when they heard anyone coming they had a habit of whirling round and round so fast that they were invisible except for the dust they raised. But from the appearance of the young one Ol' Paul had in camp, I should imagine that when full grown they'd stand about seven feet high, with a body about the size of a coal-oil drum, and covered with rough fur. The hind legs were like those of a horse, except that they were grown together at the fetlock, and ended in a single iron-shod hoof. The front legs looked more like skinny arms, or like baseball bats, with large, coarse hands on the ends of them. These arms were so long that when the animal stood at ease it rested its wrists on the ground.

The habit of the Whimpus was to station itself in the middle of a tote road, and when it heard anything coming it started whirling, the big hands flying round and round with terrible force. As it was then invisible, the unsuspecting animal walked right up to it and was spattered to a gelatin by the baseball-bat arms. This gelatin the Whimpus licked off at leisure. It usually fed on bear, elk, oxen, and such, but occasionally a lumberjack got caught.

Ol' Paul used the young one he had to mighty good advantage one winter, digging wells. He would fasten a sixteen-inch post-hole auger to the thing's hoof and set him down where he wanted a well. The Whimpus, of course, would start whirling and bore himself right down into the ground. Paul kept a rope with a swivel in it tied on to the auger, and when the well was deep enough, he'd haul him back to the surface with a windlass. But one day the swivel stuck and caused the rope to twist in two. With nothing to stop him, the little Whimpus kept right on going down, and was never seen again.

And then there was the Gumberoo, a mighty weird-looking animal that Ol' Paul came across shortly after he finished logging off the Upside Down Country.

The beast had long arms like an ape, and a round head attached to what was practically no neck at all. His body was almost the exact shape and size of the pot-bellied stoves used to heat the bunkhouse, with a tough, shiny skin. Ordinarily he walked on a pair of stubby little legs that ended in three eagle claws clenched around an iron ball. Of course, these legs weren't built for speed, but were mighty fine for wading round the rubbish dumps back of deserted towns and camps, where the animals were in the habit of feeding.

Around his middle the Gumberoo had sixteen pairs of other legs that stuck out at right angles to his body. They were very springy and strong, and he used them when for any reason he needed to really make time. In order to get a rolling start he had to get to the top of a hill, which he usually did by swinging himself through the trees by his arms. This was slow, but faster than the stove-leg gait. But once he got to the top of the hill, he would throw himself as far out and down as possible, to land on his side. This put the sixteen pairs of rubber legs under him, and he just rolled over and over, from one pair to the other, faster than the human eye could follow, which probably explains why there is no record of anyone having seen one in motion.

Ol' Paul discovered that the hides from the middle legs made fine boots, being as how they were waterproof. These were first called gumberoo boots, but later the

name was shortened to just plain gum boots. This name is used today by the makers of rubber boots worn by farmers, fishermen, sailors, and such. But the genuine gumberoo boots are scarce now, what with the Gumberoos getting extinct and all. Occasionally some fisherman comes in and reports finding part of a Gumberoo carcass, but so far it has always turned out that he has hooked onto an old rubber boot and mistaken it for part of a Gumberoo leg.

I have been told that one time Ol' Paul had a herd of them that he had domesticated. That way he was sure of a ready supply of gumberoo boots. Every spring the herders would have a big rodeo and brand the Gumberoos with the foot sizes, so that when Paul sent word he wanted a few pairs of size eleven boots or whatever, they knew exactly which Gumberoo to catch. But the winter the red-hot blizzard blew in from Texas, the Gumberoos all caught fire, being very inflammable. And as far as I know, that was the end of them.

Why There Are No Trees on the Desert

For many years in his spare time Ol' Paul had fooled around crossbreeding plants in a small way. At first he tried to cross an apple tree, a yellow pine, and a sawmill to get a tree that would keep the best features of all three. The idea was that if he could have a tree that would grow lumber already cut, the boards hanging like apples, he could get rid of all his loggers and hire apple or apricot pickers instead. Which of course would be a big saving, as everyone knows that fruit pickers work cheaper than lumberjacks, and feed themselves, which in itself is no small item. Besides that, he could deal direct with the consumer, as the Plankavos, as he hoped to call them, would do away with the sawmills, except for the few needed to provide sawdust for butcher shops and saloons.

I don't know exactly what ever happened to the Plankavo, but while he was fooling around he somehow accidentally crossed a Douglas fir, a California redwood, and a desert cactus. The tree he got was as tall as a redwood, the wood couldn't be told from fir, and it grew well in the driest desert. The main trouble was the fact that it had thorns seventy feet long, instead of branches. This made Ol' Paul sore, so he didn't breed any more trees.

However, a great many years later these trees had grown to a great size, covering the desert with a deep forest.

One day Ol' Paul gets a letter from the Government telling him he'll have to log the desert off. It seems that the Tired Eastern Business Women going out there for their vacations were complaining that they couldn't see the desert because of the trees, and the cowboys on the dude ranches were all the time coming home with their clothes snagged up by the thorns. Along with the letter is a hand-painted picture, showing him what the Government thinks a desert should look like.

As soon as Paul gets the letter he hitches Babe to the south end of the section of land the camp is on, and hauls it down to Nevada. He often moved camp this way as it was quicker than any other, and besides, the men never got homesick for the old camp.

Next morning he takes a look at the timber and knows he's in for plenty of trouble for sure, on account of those seventy-foot thorns. At first they try to tunnel under the thorns and cut the trees off at the roots, but the thorns keep the trees from falling over even after they're cut off.

Then he decides to dynamite, and what a job that is! First they dig out a powder chamber under the roots, then carry in four thousand five hundred and four cases of dynamite and two thousand and four cans of giant powder. The idea is to blast off a township at a time. All the time the heat is affecting the men something fierce, so they can only work in four-hour shifts. Even working shifts day and night and holidays, it takes three weeks and nine days to get the giant blast ready. The last case of dynamite is packed, the percussion caps are wired, and the men all move back out of danger. Ol' Paul looks around and hollers: "Let her go!"

Well sir, the shock throws every man in camp flat on his back, knocks the cupolas off three barns in Iowa, and the smoke and dust go up in a column thirty-four miles high. When the air clears somewhat the men see there's nothing left but the holes. The trees've been blown clean out of sight. As it's nearly supper time, Ol' Paul says they might as well knock off for the day, but first he reaches up and feels around on top of the smoke column, which is still standing. He finds half a wagon load of wild ducks laying up there.

It seems that a big flock had been flying over when the blast went off. It has shot the air full of sand the exact size of bird shot and killed them all instantly, except one drake who was flying well in the lead. The sand missed him, but the force of the blast put a curl in his tail feathers that has never come out.

That night the men go to bed with their stomachs full of roast duck, and naturally very well satisfied. But the next morning when they go out, they find the trees fallen back to the ground, right side up and in the holes where they were before!

There seems to be nothing for Paul to do but give the men a day off and figure what to do. The trees couldn't be cut down. They couldn't be blasted down. They had been fire-proofed the Year of the Dry Rains, and couldn't be burned down. Ol' Paul chews his nails down to the quick and still can't figure what to do. He thinks and thinks. He thinks standing up, then he thinks sitting down, but this isn't so good as the ground is too hot. So he goes and sits down in the shade of the black-smith shop and starts whittling.

He whittles a full-rigged clipper ship, full size, and tries all afternoon to get it inside a beer bottle, like the old sailors do. He gets so interested in this business that he forgets about his real problem until near supper time, and never does get the blamed thing into the bottle. So the next morning he gives the men another day off and goes into his office and thinks without whittling. Even so, it is three days before he comes tearing out with his arms full of blueprints, hollering for the straw bosses to get the men together. He's going to make a speech.

"Boys," he says, "the Gov'ment's dependin' on us. If we fail, them plans is blowed higher'n Gilroy's kite. We'll build the biggest pile-driver ever seen. And by the Great Ringtailed Catamount, we'll drive them trees down like tent pegs!'"

You see, this idea would make a story to be told in every camp this side of Mexico. Ol' Paul liked to do a job like that occasionally, even if there was no profit in it, just to remind folks he was no ordinary logger.

For thirty-nine weeks they work on the great pile-driver. It stands so high that the clouds going by are all the time knocking the upper half off, so he puts a hinge in the middle and lets the upper half down when he sees a cloud coming. For a weight he uses one of the Rocky Mountain peaks. (When he gets done he tosses it up into Colorado, where it sets to this day, right behind Colorado Springs.)

When everything is ready, they set the machine up over a thorn tree, and Babe, grunting mightily, hauls the weight to the top. It comes down and strikes with a crash that is heard for one hundred and three miles. The tree is driven clear to bed rock, its top being sixteen feet below the ground.

Ol' Paul reckons that'll do, and they go to work in real earnest. The noise and dust are terrific, as they drive a tree every three minutes, and Babe is sweating from every pore. The sweat pours down off his sides and down his legs and runs in streams across the desert. It washes big gullies in the soft soil that can be seen to this day. These streams running every which way hinder the work, so Paul grabs a shovel and digs a ditch for them to drain into. This is now known as the Grand Canyon. After Paul left the country the Government ran the Colorado River through it.

As soon as he gets the pile-driver crew working smoothly, Paul goes back to camp to catch up with a number of smaller problems that've piled up while he's

busy with the cactus trees. On account of the heat, the men want ice tea for every meal, and the cooks need ice to keep the meat from spoiling. But there's no ice to be had.

Suddenly Ol' Paul remembers something. That, by the way, was one of the secrets of his success, that habit of remembering things even when they didn't seem worth remembering at the time.

It seems that while they had been building the pile-driver, Babe had been allowed to run loose, and had come back from Alaska with a small snowstorm snagged on one horn. Paul had taken it off, and having no use for a snowstorm round camp at the time, had put it in an old sheep pen in a dry lake-bed a few miles from camp, and forgotten it completely.

So now he decides to go and see how it's getting along. He sort of expects to find it pretty much wilted from the heat, but instead he finds the dry lake frozen from bank to bank. In the center of it the snowstorm's dug a burrow, and is as happy as a clam. Paul breaks off a piece of the ice and finds that it's much colder than ordinary ice, and when it melts it leaves a dry spot. This puzzles him a bit, then he sees that it's dry ice. Naturally, if you freeze a dry lake you can get nothing but dry ice from it—it stands to reason. So Paul keeps the snowstorm there all the time he's logging off the desert, and the cooks never have to worry about the icebox pans running over.

Building the Rockies

A couple of years after Ol' Paul finished logging off the Great Plains to furnish grazing land for the buffalo, he gets a letter from the King of Sweden, saying as how he has more Swedes than he has room for over there, and he wonders if Paul knows of any place where he can send some of them.

Right away Ol' Paul thinks of North Dakota and Minnesota, and writes the King a letter describing the two places. The King writes back that Minnesota sounds fine, but that he wants North Dakota logged off, so his people can raise wheat. Also he wonders if the hills could be taken off, as these folks have been raised near the water and are used to being able to see a long way.

After a good deal of dickering they come to some kind of an agreement, and Paul gets ready to start operations. There's a considerable number of things he has to do, however, before he can actually start logging. First of all he has to get rid of the Huggags.

These were huge beasts standing about thirteen feet high, and weighing a little over three tons. Their heads were bald and bumpy, with long, warty snouts, and floppy ears about the size of gunny sacks. Instead of hair, they were thinly covered with pine needles, and pitch all the time oozed from every pore, due to their feeding on pitch-pine knots. But the queerest thing about them was the fact that they had no knee or hock joints, which kept them from lying down. So when they got ready to sleep, the whole herd faced in one direction, usually the northwest. Then each one picked a handy tree, and after bracing his big splayed feet solidly against the ground, would lean to the left against the tree, go to sleep, and snore quietly. Such a weight naturally made the trees lean some, and in certain places you'll still find them all bent one way.

So Paul sends a crew in to their bed grounds to trap them out. At first they try to catch them in bear traps, but the Huggag's feet are too big. And hunting them is no good, because at the first sign of danger they raise the pine needles in their hides, like porcupines, and can't be told from a pile of slashings. So the men get busy and hunt up the favorite Huggag sleeping trees, which are easy to find because of their lean, and saw them halfway through. When the Huggags lean against them for their nap, the weakened trunks snap, and they fall flat on their sides. Having no joints, they're unable to get up, once they're down, so are helpless until the lumberjacks come back. In this way they're soon most all trapped out, and are very scarce now, although occasionally they come down around deserted farms and sleep against the buildings, causing them to lean, too.

The next problem is that there are no rivers big enough to float logs, so Ol' Paul has to get out the sections of the Whistling River he's been saving and lay them out where they'll do the most good. This takes quite some time, as of course you can't lay a river out like a carpet. The land has to be surveyed and a lot of things like that.

However, he finally gets everything taken care of, and by the time the first snow falls he's all ready to start work. Besides his regular woods crew he has seven axemen that the King of Sweden sent over to help out.

They're not much for looks, but before the winter's over their fame has spread all through the timber country. They are huge fellows, and all brothers, and have worked out a special system for felling trees. They work side by side going up hill, mowing down trees twenty-five at a swing. Naturally, by the time they reach the top of a hill their axes are mighty dull. But instead of going back to camp to grind them, they each pick out a big rock at the top and start it rolling. As it rolls and bounces down the hill, they follow, taking enormous strides and grinding their axes as they run.

With a crew like this work goes on at a great rate, and by spring the whole country is logged off, and the slashings piled up ready to burn. In the meantime Ol' Paul and the King have been doing quite a lot of writing back and forth. The King offers Paul a bonus if he'll drive the logs to Sweden, and makes a side bet of a dollar and a half that it can't be done. Paul says as how his men can drive logs anywhere, so he puts his best river crew on the job, with Shot Gunderson in charge.

Ol' Paul goes with them through the Great Lakes and helps them get the drive down Niagara Falls. This was really quite a chore, as the falls were much higher then than they are now. But they get the entire drive over in three days and never lose a log. The trip down the rest of the St. Lawrence River and across the Atlantic is comparatively simple. They make it in three weeks, in spite of having to stop in the English Channel while the King comes out in a rowboat to see what an American log drive looks like.

While the men are gone with the logs Ol' Paul's been busy getting rid of the hills. He has Ole build a big sledge hammer and pounds the hills out flat as flapjacks. When that's done he cuts some of the rivers down to creeks and runs them here and there to make the country look nice. Then he writes the King of Sweden to send over one of his Prime Ministers to O. K. the job.

A few months later the King's favorite Prime Minister arrives, and Paul has one of his men drive him out over the country in a buckboard. And it is really a beautiful

job. As far as the eye can see is rich flat land covered with long green grass. The Prime Minister is very well pleased with it except for one thing. At that time there were no mountains between the Dakotas and the Pacific, and in the winter the winds blew in from Siberia and made the country mighty cold. So the Prime Minister tells Paul that he will have to put up some sort of a wind-break before the King will send him his check.

That kind of puts Ol' Paul up a stump, as a thing of that size is a pretty big order even for him. But he goes over and studies the lay of the land and figures a while. It's plain to be seen that an ordinary board fence will not do, as it'll cost a fortune just to keep it in repair, even if he can build one high enough to do any good.

While out looking the country over he finds a de-serted prairie-dog town. Now Ol' Paul always has an eye out for anything new that he can use in his business, so he pulls a few of the old prairie-dog holes up and takes them back to camp, intending to saw them up for post holes or something.

That night, however, having stopped in the cookshack for a bite to eat before going to bed, he's watching Sour-dough Sam setting his sourdough for next morning, when he gets an idea that probably is the best one he ever had. He doesn't explain it to anyone, but gets busy and has a small cookshack built on sled runners, with holes in the bottom.

The next morning he has Sam move his sourdough crocks and part of his helpers into it. Then he hitches Babe onto the outfit and hauls it out to the prairie-dog town. When they get there, he drives along slower, and Sam and the helpers get busy filling up the prairie-dog holes with sourdough, pouring it into them through the holes in the floor. Ole, the Big Swede, follows and plugs the holes with blocks of wood after they're filled.

It takes them most all day to work their way down from Alaska to New Mexico, but when they finish, every hole is filled clear to the top. If you've had any experience with sourdough, you can imagine what happens when all that sourdough starts to rise. The ground shakes and heaves for days. Big cracks show up on the prairie, and great rocks are pushed up. Inside of a week there's as fine a range of mountains as anyone could wish for, standing on the site of the old prairie-dog town.

The King of Sweden is so pleased that he sends Paul a bonus of two dollars along with the check for the job.

That sourdough hasn't quit working yet, especially out around the Jackson Hole country, where it can be heard gurgling and rumbling around under the ground, and occasionally causing water to shoot up to a great height.

Johnny Inkslinger

Soon after Ol' Paul invented mass production in the logging business and got the system to working right, he found himself in a peck of trouble. It seems that the logging went so fast he couldn't begin to keep up with his office work.

At that time there were no figures as we know them now. So he has to do all his figuring in his head and keep all his records there too. It takes eight days and forty-seven hours to figure the payroll alone, and that's only the beginning. There are the commissary accounts, the logging records, hay and grain bills, and a thousand and one other things.

His fingers get blistered from counting on them, but

he doesn't stop, and new blisters form and push the old ones back towards his wrists, and still he keeps on counting. Finally the tips of his fingers are blistered clear to his elbows. Luckily, they have time to get well by the time they reach the elbows, so go no farther. But strain as he may, he can never get more than half done.

In desperation he takes some time off and goes up to the North Pole, where he had left the Day-Stretcher he'd invented when he was logging off the Arctic. (Afterwards he'd sold it to the Eskimos, they being so pleased with the long nights it gave them.) Arriving there, he gives old chief Fancypants a broken jackknife and a lead quarter to stretch a sackful of days he's brought with him. He only has them stretched to twice the usual length, being as how he's in quite a sweat to get back to camp, and doesn't want to wait.

As it turns out, this is just as well, for he finds that when he tries to use them he's worse off than before. Naturally, if he was getting behind with the figuring when he worked an ordinary day, it stands to reason that working twice as long a day, he'd get just twice as far behind. And that's exactly what happened, so after a few days he has to give the idea up.

However, he doesn't throw those extra long days out. But being very thrifty, he ships them to a second-hand dealer in the East who has been peddling them out ever since. Perhaps you yourself can remember days that seemed endless, especially of a Monday. If so, you may be sure that it was just one of those days. Almost every school and business has a supply of them.

But to get back to Paul's problem. He's in a stew, sure enough! It looks as though he'll have to invent mass production for figuring the same as he's done for logging. But seeing as how it takes a certain amount of time for even Paul to invent inventions, and him being so busy, he thinks he'll first look around camp and see if he can find someone who can help him.

Here he runs into trouble. He finds a top loader who can figure a little, but Shot Gunderson, the woods boss, insists that he can't be spared from the woods, seeing as how he hasn't any too many top loaders as it is. Then there's the fellow in the cookshack helping Hot Biscuit Slim, who's been heard to say he can both spell and cipher. But Sam lets it be known, in no uncertain terms, that dreadful things will probably find their way into the food if his helpers are interfered with. And not even Paul dares rile a camp cook.

So it looks like the only thing left is to try and teach Backward Bill Barber, the bull cook, to figure. You see, a fellow that's no good for anything else is given the job of carrying wood and water for the cooks, and looking after the bunkhouses. He's called the bull cook, for no good reason that I ever heard of. Naturally he can very easily be replaced, so Backward Bill gets the job. It's surprising how often people like Backward Bill get put into important jobs because they can be so easily replaced where they are.

For a while he seems to do all right. But soon Paul discovers that the figures never come out in anything but odd numbers, and finds that Bill has had a finger cut off at some time, which throws his counting into nines instead of tens. Being an odd number, nine is much harder to figure with than ten. So that finishes Backward Bill as a figurer.

Next Ol' Paul tries a crude system of bookkeeping by means of notches chopped in trees. On one tree he chops payroll notches, and on another commissary bills, and so on. For a time he keeps a crew of men busy chopping notches as he calls out the numbers. He gets so he can call out three numbers at once, and that's something not everyone can do. This system works fairly well for a time, although Paul hates to keep so many men out of the woods. But these men, not being real figurers, make many mistakes. A notch-chopper chopping payroll notches'll climb a timber record tree by mistake, or a commissary notch-chopper'll get onto a hay and grain

tree, and soon the records get as badly mixed as before.

So again he's right back where he started from. He's losing sleep and weight from worrying, and even then he isn't really getting it all done, as he's so busy with other things. And he has so many notch-chopping crews out that he's kind of lost track of them and isn't at all sure that he's called them all in. He's haunted by the fear that maybe he's left a crew out in the woods somewhere to starve.

For a while he thinks seriously about going back to the great cave where he grew up, and spending the rest of his life whittling. I think this was the only time that any problem threatened to be more than Ol' Paul could solve. He kept getting thinner and thinner, and he didn't even have the heart to comb his great beard any more. It is said that the mess-hall was thrown into an uproar one morning at breakfast when two full-grown bobcats chased a snowshoe rabbit out of his whiskers. But that may or may not be true.

He gets in the habit of roaming the woods at night, with the faithful Ox at his heels, just worrying. One morning, finding himself in a part of the country that is strange to him, he decides to explore a little before going back to camp. (Although he doesn't know it, he is near Boston, which everyone knows is the seat of Learning, Culture, and Baked Beans. However, it is unlikely that he'd have cared even if he had known, as he's already learned practically everything there is to know. He's not interested in culture, and beans are no novelty to a logger.)

About ten-thirty he's sitting on a low hill, resting, when he's startled by a yell that uproots trees all around him. Up to that time he's supposed that he's the only man that can holler loud enough to knock down trees, so he's more than somewhat curious.

He stands up and steps over a couple of small mountains, and gets the surprise of his life. Sitting on a hill is a fellow almost as large as Paul himself. He has a high, smooth forehead, and instead of wearing a fur cap he's bareheaded, which even then was a sign of high learning. But the thing that takes Paul's eye is the collar. It is very high, stiff, and pure white, and looks very uncomfortable. (It is said that after he went to work for Paul he kept a crew of thirty-nine men busy every Sunday whitewashing it.)

The strange giant is busy scraping the limestone bluff on the other side of the river with a jackknife the size of a four-horse double-tree, scattering the pieces for miles around. When the rock is smooth enough to suit him, he takes an enormous pencil from behind his ear and starts writing down columns of queer marks with it. The pencil is over three feet in diameter and seventy-six feet long —the first one ever used.

Paul stands around, first on one foot and then on the

other, waiting for him to look up so he can find out who he is and what he's doing. But it seems that the fellow has just invented concentration and is busy practicing it as he works. So of course he never bats an eye when Paul shuffles his feet, knocking down thirty-five acres of standing timber. Nor does he seem to hear when Paul says, "Reckon as how it's goin' to be a mighty dry summer if it don't rain soon." As I said before, he was concentrating, and concentrating is a mighty exacting operation when it's done right.

After a while, however, he finishes what he's doing and turns around to look at Paul. But he still says nothing, and Paul says the same thing, as the white collar has him impressed more than somewhat. So Paul gets out his can of Copenhagen and offers the stranger a chaw; then they both sit and squirt tobacco juice at ants for a bit until they raise the river almost to flood stage. After they discuss the chances of rain, Paul asks him what he's

doing with the marks on the cliff. (He thinks maybe they're some kind of pictures.)

The fellow tells him he's Johnny Inkslinger and those are figures. But naturally Paul knows that figures are something that you think but can't see.

"Them is figures, and I'm sole owner and inventor of them," Johnny insists.

He shows Paul a little of how they work, even working out a couple of problems that Paul thinks up, and finally convinces him that they really work. Then Paul wants to know what he figures, and is completely flabbergasted when Johnny tells him that he just figures for the fun of it, as he has everything that needs figuring all figured.

Paul can't imagine a full-grown man sitting around all day figuring just for the fun of it, but Johnny tells him that he always liked it. As he grew older he got dissatisfied with just figuring in his head as everyone else did, so one day he sat down and instead of just sitting, he sat and thought about what he could do to make figuring more fun.

Finally he hit on the idea of inventing figures that could be seen as well as thought. He worked for many months, and the result was a system whereby he could not only figure anything, but see the figures at the same time. Moreover, figures figured this way could be written down in books and saved for future reference. (This is the system now used in all our schools.)

As you can well imagine, Ol' Paul is pretty excited by this time. Here is mass production in figures, the same as he has in logging. And the fellow seems to be a real artist, so probably could be hired for practically nothing. If he can get Johnny to work for him his worries will be over and he can get out in the woods again. So he puts on the expression a man wears when he holds a royal flush and wants to give the other fellow the impression he's bluffing on a pair of deuces, and asks Johnny how he'd like to have a job figuring for him.

Johnny reckons that would be mighty fine, but that he's a poor man and can't afford such luxuries. Finally Paul convinces him that he means it when he says that he'll furnish him with all the figuring he can do, besides giving him books to write them in, and pay him thirty dollars a month. He right away starts off for camp at a run, he's that anxious to begin work. He was the first bookkeeper in history, and his job with Ol' Paul lasted for many years to the great advantage of both.

The Baby Rainstorm
or,
MORE ABOUT THE RAIN
THAT CAME STRAIGHT UP

One spring, a good many years back, Ol' Paul had him a logging camp on the headwaters of the River That Ran Sidewise. He'd had a profitable winter and the landings were jammed full of logs decked up waiting for the spring floods to float them down to the mills.

Finally the weather turned warm and the snow started to melt. A few more days and the ice would break up so they could get the drive under way. Then one morning the men woke up to find it was raining. Now rain is not so unusual at that time of year, but this is no ordinary rain!

As everybody knows, ordinary rain falls down, but this rain fell UP! All over camp, and for as far around as anyone could see, streams of big raindrops were squirting up out of the ground, sailing straight up in the air and disappearing in the clouds overhead!

And that brought trouble. For, like I say, folks are used to the kind of rain that comes down and build their houses to take care of that kind, seldom giving the other kind a thought. And that was the case with Ol' Paul's camp. The buildings all had tight roofs that water couldn't come through, but the floors, on the other hand, were made with wide cracks so that water and mud tracked in by the lumberjacks would run through to the ground below.

But now, with the rain coming up, the floors leaked like sieves and the water gathered on the ceilings and couldn't leak out. By the time the men woke up there were four feet of water on the underside of the ceiling of every bunkhouse in camp, and it was getting deeper every minute. The men as they got up had to duck their heads to keep from bumping into the water.

One of the loggers hotfooted it over to Paul's office to tell him about it.

"Paul!" he hollered when he could get his breath. "The rain is a-comin' straight up this morning!"

"Yuh means it's a-clabberin' up to rain, don't yuh?" Paul asked, as he hunted under his bunk for his socks. "Why the Sam Hill don't yuh learn to say what yuh mean."

"Nossir!" the lumberjack insisted. "I meant jest what I said, that the rain is a-comin' straight up outta the ground and yuh kin take a look fer yerself!"

And to prove it he hauled back the big bearskin rug that had been keeping the rain from coming up through the floor of Paul's office. When he did that streams of water shot up through the cracks and started spattering on the ceiling overhead. Before he could put it back Paul's bed and his clothes were all soaked and he knew he had a sure enough problem on his hands this time.

Ol' Paul and the lumberjack sat in the middle of the rug where it was fairly dry, and thought about what to do. Every so often Paul would stomp over to the window and look out. He couldn't seem to believe his eyes, and he tried looking out with the window closed, and he tried looking out with the window open, and later he even went outside for a good close look. But anyway he looked at it, the rain was sure enough coming straight up!

Meanwhile, the lumberjacks over in the bunkhouses, and the stable bucks and the bull cooks and the mess hall flunkeys were all in a very bad humor. The cooks were in a bad humor too, but camp cooks are almost always that way, so nobody noticed any particular difference in them.

After a while a delegation came to Ol' Paul and told him that he'd better do something about this business pretty soon or they'd all quit and go to work for Sow-belly Burke, his hated rival.

Ol' Paul assured them that he'd get to the bottom of the mystery as soon as possible, but pointed out that it would take time, since nothing like it had ever happened before. That being the case, there was of course nothing written in the books about how to deal with it, so he'd have to figure it all out by himself.

"Besides," he told them, "think of the stories you can tell in the towns this summer, about how you got your drive out in spite of the rain that fell straight up!"

But they were still mad and going to quit, so he saw he'd have to take measures, and pretty quick, at that.

After a spell of unusually heavy thinking he sent the lumberjack to get Johnny Inkslinger, and to have him bring a mail order catalogue from his favorite mail order house.

When Johnny got there Paul started looking through the catalogue while he explained to Johnny that a feller's clothes were made for ordinary rain, sorta like he was shingled over.

When Johnny looked kind of undecided Paul went on to explain that a feller's hat stuck out over his collar to keep the rain from running down his neck, and his coat overlapped his britches and his britches overlapped his boots. But with rain like this, falling up instead of down, it fell straight up his britches legs, straight up his sleeves, and up under his coat and hat. It was no wonder the lumberjacks were in such a bad humor.

Johnny agreed with that, but couldn't see what could be done about it beyond putting all their clothes on upside down, and that didn't seem to be practical.

Paul told him he had the answer. He wanted an order sent off right away for bumbershoots, enough for two for every man in camp, including the stable bucks and bull cooks. And he showed Johnny the picture in the catalogue. Johnny told him what he was looking at was "umbrellas," and that anyway they would do no good being as they were made for rain that fell down, while this rain was falling up.

Paul allowed he knew as well as the next man what

bumbershoots were used for but he wanted them ordered, and marked "Rush" at that.

A couple days later the bumbershoots came, two for every man jack in camp, and you should have heard the lumberjacks roar. No self-respecting lumberjack had ever been known to carry one of the sissy things and they weren't going to start it now. They might be all right for city dudes, but not for reg'lar he-lumberjacks! No sir! They'd quit first.

Ol' Paul goes on helping Ole open the boxes and tells the lumberjacks to keep their shirts on a minute till they see what he has in mind.

As fast as the bumbershoots are unpacked the little chore boy opens them up and Ol' Paul takes his jack-knife and cuts the handles off short inside and fastens on a couple of snowshoe loops instead. When he has them all fixed up he has Johnny call the roll. As each logger comes up Paul hands him a couple of the remodeled bumbershoots and tells him to slip his feet in the loops. The first fellers are a mite shy about the business, but

after they put them on and straddle off, like they were wearing snowshoes, they find that the durn things do keep the rain from coming up their pantlegs. And from then on the men push and holler for the line ahead to hurry up so they can get theirs.

"See there," says Ol' Paul. "I guess I knowed what I was doing. Don't reckon there is anything sissy about wearin' bumbershoots on your feet. An' anyways we'll call 'em bumbershoes from now on, jest to be sure!"

The men all cheered again, and decided not to quit after all.

The next morning a friendly Indian, Chief Rink-tumdiddy by name, came tearing in to camp wanting to see Paul. He told Ol' Paul that he and another Indian were out hunting the day before and camped by the mouth of a cave out on the prairie a way. After they'd eaten their supper they decided to explore this cave, so they took along some pine knots for torches, and started out. They go back through the narrow twisting passages for about half a mile, as near as they can judge, when all of a sudden they hear the goshawfullest noise they've ever laid an ear next to. They don't stop to argue, but tear outta there as fast as they can hyper. They figger that by going in there they've made the Great Spirit mad, and that it was him they heard hollering. So now this Indian wants Paul to see if he can talk the Great Spirit out of his mad.

Ol' Paul is plumb curious, but from what the Chief tells him he knows, the cave is too small for him to get into, and he hasn't Babe along to burrow for him, so he sits still and thinks for a spell. Finally he allows as how that maybe two fellers listening together could listen far enough back to hear the noise from the mouth of the cave. That sounded like a good idea, but the Indian was plumb scared to go back, so Paul called Chris Crosshaul to come along instead.

The cave wasn't hard to find, and when they got there they both listened as hard as they could and sure enough, they could just hear the noise. But when they tried listening separately they couldn't hear a sound.

For a while Paul listens to the rumpus he can hear going on back in the cave, and a very curious sound it is, too. It's sorta mixed up with whimpering and whining like a lost puppy, mixed in with dribbling, splashing sounds, and a sort of pattering, and now and again a hollow booming like lightning might sound if it was shut in a cellar.

After a spell of especially hard listening that left them

both red in the face and out of breath, Paul turns to Chris and allows that what they hear is nothing in the wide world but a baby rainstorm that's got itself lost back in the cave, and is bellering for his maw!

"Yuh don't say," says Chris, doubtful-like.

"Yessir!" says Paul, "An' by lookin' at my pocket compass I've discovered that the noise is a-comin' from right under our lumbercamp! The way I figger it, that little feller got separated from the rest of the herd and got in here by mistake a while back. Now, he's lost and scared. You jest heerd him whimperin' and thunderin' his little heart out back in there. Chances are he's got all upset in the dark and is rainin' straight up instead of down and don't know it. We gotta get him outta there."

"Yeah?" says Chris Crosshaul. "It sounds reasonable, but how the Sam Hill we gonna git him out?"

"Well, here's the way I see it," says Ol' Paul, when they had their pipes going good. "The only way to git that critter outta there is to call him out. It's a cinch we can't drag him out because there's no way to get a-hold of a critter like that. And nobody ever had any luck tryin' to chase a rainstorm anywheres that I ever heard tell about."

"Reckon you're right that fur, Paul," says Chris, "but I never hear tell of anyone that can call a rainstorm, neither."

"That's the beauty of the whole thing," says Paul. "We'll be the first ones to ever do such a thing."

"Jest how do you figger to go about it," Chris wants to know. "Yuh don't mean to tell me you kin holler like rainstorms, do yuh?"

"Not right now, I can't," says Paul. "But I figger I kin durn soon learn. Yuh see, I know a feller in Kansas City that will rent yuh all kinds of disguises. I'll git him to disguise me up to look like a rainstorm, then I'll go out and live with a tribe of them and learn their language. Should be simple enough, shouldn't it?"

And that's just what he did. He went and got himself duded up in a rainstorm suit till you wouldn't have known him. Then he went out into Iowa where most of the rainstorms summered. He fell in with a big tribe of them, and his disguise was so perfect that they just figgered he was a strange rainstorm, maybe blowed up from Texas way, and invited him to stay with them as long as he liked.

He had a mighty fine time all summer, helping them rain out open-air political rallies and the like, although I think he took an unfair advantage at times, being as how he always got the crowd he was with to rain out the fellers he didn't want to see elected, while they stayed away from the rallies of the fellers he liked.

But anyways, late in the summer he came back. Just to show off, he was all the time throwing rainstorm words into his talk, until the lumberjacks hardly knew what he was talking about. Then one day he went over to the mouth of the cave where the rainstorm was, and getting down on his hands and knees he put his face up close to the entrance of the cave and imitated the cry a mother rainstorm makes when she is calling her young ones.

As soon as he did that, the noise and thundering and blubbering stopped sudden. There wasn't a sound to be heard, and the rain, for the first time all summer, stopped coming up around camp.

"See that," says Paul, with a big grin. And then he hollered the rainstorm holler again, and that little rainstorm came a-tearing outta that cave like he'd been sent for and couldn't come. He was just a little feller compared to what some rainstorms are, and a mite puny looking from being shut in the dark for so long. He jumps into Ol' Paul's arms and licks his face and rains all over him like an excited puppy dog.

Ol' Paul pets him and talks to him soothing like, till he kinda quiets down, then sends him off down to Iowa where the rest of the rainstorms are. The last we saw of him he was just a little cloud over in the next county, and plumb busted out with rainbows, he was so tickled.

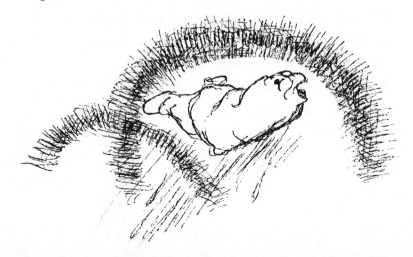

The Giant Bullsnake

Now Knute was by no means an ordinary snake. He was never content to be just ordinary—he wanted to be the greatest snake that ever was. From the time he was just a little fellow, he was all the time taking stretching exercises to develop his muscles. So he grew very fast, and it is said that when he was three years old, he was able, with his bare tail, to lasso and hogtie a full-grown buffalo bull, and that is something that most snakes cannot do even when they are much older.

When he was full-grown, he was so long that when he was taking a drink out of one of the Great Lakes his tail, likely as not, was scaring the daylights out of homesteaders out by where McCook, Nebraska, now is. What we now call the Great Plains was once his bed ground. Tossing in his sleep over the course of some centuries, he wore down the trees to sagebrush and smoothed off the hills as we know them now.

During the Indian wars Knute joined up with Custer's army, where a missionary taught him to talk. He was quite a pet with the men because of the tall tales he could spin of the things he'd seen here and there. But he scared the Indians so bad that the soldiers never could catch them, and he was so big that the General was afraid he'd accidentally squash a bunch of men some day, so he asked him please to leave, which was all right with Knute, he being very accommodating. Anyway, he was getting a little tired of army life.

So he went off up into the Badlands in South Dakota, where no one much lived at that time, to be a hermit. For a while he was quite happy there, game being plentiful, so he had plenty of time to think. Not that he had anything special to think about, but he just liked to think.

However, one day when he was prowling around near Laramie, Wyoming, he came across a railroad track, the first one he'd ever seen. He thought it was some kind of varmint trail, so he sat himself down to wait for the varmint. Directly along came a freight train a mile and a quarter long, with two engines—and he swallowed the whole thing.

The train crew jumped in time to save themselves, but what a time they had trying to make the boss believe their story when they explained the loss of their train. Finally the boss fined them each a dollar and a quarter. Being as train men were kinda hard to get those days, he hated to fire them.

But poor Knute! It was easy enough for him to digest the freight cars, which were loaded with meat for the army posts, but when he finally digested the boilers, all that steam turned loose in his stomach gave him a bad stomach-ache. At first the steam had a pressure of one hundred and ninety pounds to the inch, just as it came from the boilers. But the indigestion gave him fever, and the fever made more steam, and so it went. Before long he had three hundred pounds pressure and it was still a-going up. He felt pretty bad.

He had to have something done, but he couldn't go to

the Indian medicine men as they were scared stiff at the sight of him. Then he thought of Paul Bunyan, the great inventor and logger. As far as anyone knows, Paul never found a problem he couldn't solve, so Knute tore out for his camp.

Paul listened to the snake's story and let out a low whistle that blew in the windows of the Sunshine Cafe in Sabinal, Texas, which wasn't there yet.

This was the kind of problem he liked. So he thought even faster than usual, but even so, he had chewed his nails till the scraps were piled round him nearly to his knees, and his hands were all tangled up in his whiskers, before he thought of anything. By that time Ole, the Big Swede, had gotten back from replacing the windows of the Sunshine Cafe, and Paul right away put him to work taking a safety valve and whistle off an old donkey engine back of the blacksmith shop. Ole was as good a plumber as ever wore hair, so he had no trouble connecting these things up to Knute's neck.

Right away the snake felt better. The valve was set to keep the pressure at one hundred and ten pounds. That was just enough to keep his stomach warm. And he was as tickled with the whistle as a kid with a new red wagon. He wanted to pay Paul for curing him but Paul wouldn't hear of it. Said he was mighty obliged to Knute for bringing him such an interesting problem. Folks all over the country would be telling that story for years.

A few days later Knute was back in camp with another little problem for Paul. He said that, what with his getting along in years, his circulation wasn't what it used to be; and his tail being so far from the rest of him, he was having considerable trouble keeping it warm. That one was nothing at all for Ol' Paul. He just had Ole run a pipe line for the steam from the whistle right down Knute's back to his tail. Along the last mile or two he fastened a lot of old steam radiators he'd picked up somewhere or other. And though that was the beginning of the coldest winter the oldest Indians could remember, Knute came through without a single chilblain.

And more than that, the heat attracted antelope, buffalo, and jack rabbits by the thousands, making his hunting a cinch.

Naturally this was the beginning of a very fine friendship that lasted for many years. Knute got into the habit of dropping into camp every now and then with a bit of fresh meat for the men's Sunday dinner. So he was right popular with everyone, even the cooks, and that was something, for it's very, very seldom that anyone is popular with a camp cook.

A couple of years later Ol' Paul was dickering with the Queen of Spain on a lumber deal. It seems that she had options on about four states that she wanted logged off. The price she offered was about right, but the time limit on the job was so short that Johnny Inkslinger, the bookkeeper, was worried and advised Paul not to try it.

But Paul just grinned in his whiskers and reckoned that he'd make out all right. He said that if he needed more men there were plenty of good ones yet in Sweden. In the meantime he just sat around whittling, and occasionally went out to the blacksmith shop where Ole, the Big Swede, and a lot of helpers were working on something in the way of a secret contraption. And Johnny was worrying himself sick.

A few days later a timber cruiser came into camp with the news that Sowbelly Burke, Paul's old enemy, had

heard of the deal, and had sent his straw boss, Mike Fink by name, to Sweden and hired all the Swedes there. Johnny was about fit to be tied by this time, but Paul just sat and whittled.

Later the same day one of Sowbelly's men came in with a message for Paul. It seems that Burke was ready to bet a dollar and a quarter that Paul couldn't finish on time. Paul sent word back that he'd take the bet and raise a quarter. This puzzled Burke, as he knew that under the terms of the contract Ol' Paul had to pay a whale of a penalty if he was late, and he had less than half enough men for a job that size.

By this time the story had spread to every lumber-camp and mill town in the country. Bets were being made everywhere on the outcome. Lots of folks thought that at last Sowbelly had gotten the best of Paul. But Paul's men stayed loyal, taking all bets. Even Hot Biscuit Slim bet a dime. But they were worried. They thought a lot of Paul, and working for him meant a lot to them.

However, a couple of weeks later, the straw bosses told the men at breakfast to pack their lunch buckets and get their axes, as work had finally started on the Queen's job.

When they came out of the mess hall, there was Knute waiting for them. But the way he was duded up was a caution. Right back of his shoulder blades were strapped two saw blades each forty feet long, and down his back were the bunks and stakes off thirty trains of log cars. And in addition to all this, there was also a donkey engine and a boom for loading logs from the ground.

Rope ladders hung down his sides and the men climbed these to find places on his back. Ole was sitting by the whistle, and when everyone was loaded, he blew the whistle twice and they tore out.

The two saw blades cut a swath through the timber like a mowing machine, and every little way they dropped a crew to top and trim the fallen timber so it would be ready to load on the way back.

That way timber was cut faster than it ever had been before. But after a few days Knute began to limp from the wear and tear of hauling such heavy loads through rough country. So Ole shod him, nailing ninety-three thousand and fourteen pairs of horse shoes on his belly scales, and from then on there was no trouble.

It was really a stirring sight to see Ol' Knute come dusting into camp at night. As far back as you could see was bend after bend of him swinging round the curves of the tote road, and on his back loads and loads of good saw logs with the men riding on top waving their fur caps and hollering. The sparks from his shoes hitting the frozen ground made a solid line of fire the full length of him. The steam flying back from his nostrils almost hid Ole, who rode on Knute's head holding a lantern and blowing the whistle every forty rods.

After they unloaded, it took nine hundred and forty-four men an hour and a quarter to rub him down and cool him out so he would not catch cold.

All winter they worked like that, and the job was finished with three days to spare, winning many bets for the men as well as bonuses all round. But Paul had to chase Sowbelly clear to the Gulf of Mexico to collect his, and then he only got about six bits, as Burke had had to pay the Swedes all winter even though they didn't work, so he was broke.

The Queen of Spain wrote Paul a long letter afterwards, and we all figgered that she probably said some mighty nice things about him, but being as how the letter was written in Spanish, we never did find out, nor did Paul. But the story of how Paul gave Sowbelly Burke his come-uppance was told for years in all the lumber-camps in the country.

It seems that Ol' Paul . . .